Journey to the Center of the CENTER of the EARTH

Acknowledgments

Artists: Penko Gelev
Sotir Gelev

First edition for North America (including Canada and Mexico), Philippine Islands, and Puerto Rico published in 2007 by Barron's Educational Series, Inc.

All inquiries should be addressed to:
Barron's Educational Series, Inc.
250 Wireless Boulevard
Hauppauge, NY 11788
www.barronseduc.com

ISBN-13 (Hardcover): 978-0-7641-5982-4
ISBN-10 (Hardcover): 0-7641-5982-8
ISBN-13 (Paperback): 978-0-7641-3495-1
ISBN-10 (Paperback): 0-7641-3495-7

Library of Congress Control No.: 2005935390

Photo credits:
p40 Roger-Viollet/TopFoto.co.uk
p47 Topham Picturepoint/TopFoto.co.uk

Every effort has been made to trace copyright holders. The Salariya Book Company apologizes for any omissions and would be pleased, in such cases, to add an acknowledgment in future editions.

Printed and bound in China
9 8 7 6 5 4 3 2 1

Journey to the Center of the Earth

JULES VERNE

illustrated by
penko gelev

BARRON'S

retold by
fiona
macdonald

series created and designed by
David Salariya

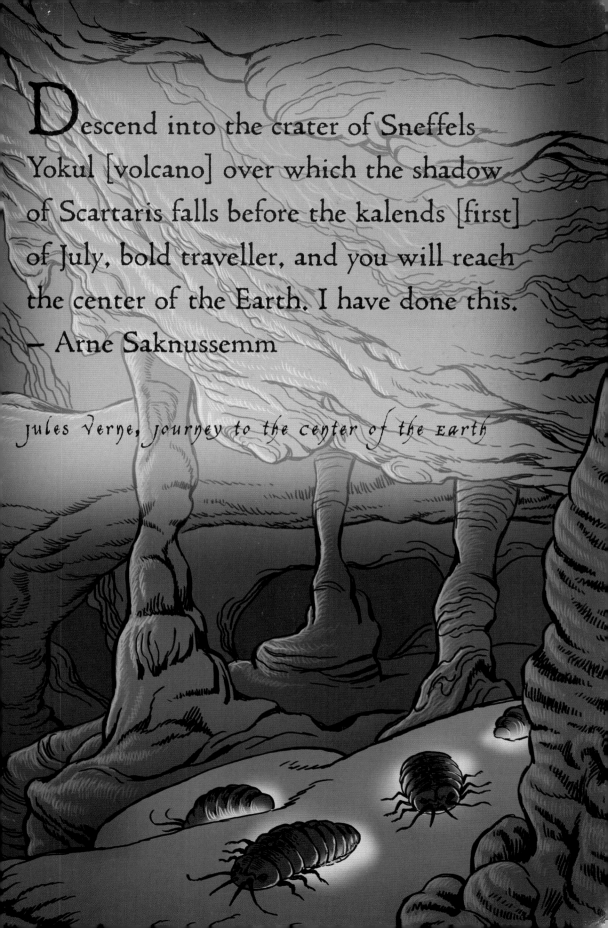

Descend into the crater of Sneffels Yokul [volcano] over which the shadow of Scartaris falls before the kalends [first] of July, bold traveller, and you will reach the center of the Earth. I have done this.
– Arne Saknussemm

Jules Verne, Journey to the Center of the Earth

CHARACTERS

Axel

Professor Otto
Lidenbrock

Arne Saknussemm

Hans

Gräuben

Martha

Mr. Fridriksson

Professor Thomson

Captain Bjarne

Baron Trampe—
Danish Governor
of Iceland.

Mr. Finsen—Mayor
of Reykjavik

"Axel, Follow Me!"

Hamburg, north Germany, May 24th, 1863

Professor Lidenbrock here already?

Axel and Martha are talking in the kitchen. It's a lazy Sunday morning, and not yet time for lunch. But they hear footsteps outside, then a door banging sharply. Martha is startled.

Why has the Professor returned so soon? And why is he so excited? The Professor—Axel's uncle—studies rocks. He's world-famous, and respected. But he's also hasty, hot-tempered—and gets carried away by wild new ideas.

In spite of his fierce temper, the Professor is kind-hearted. He looks after Axel, whose parents are dead, and Gräuben, his goddaughter. They live in his old, untidy house, and help him with his studies. Martha cooks for them.

Martha is right! It is the Professor coming home! He's in a great hurry, as usual. He rushes into the house without stopping to take off his coat. Then he runs up to his study, calling loudly for Axel.

Axel, follow me!

A Mysterious Message

Axel finds the Professor seated in his favorite chair, close to the study window. He's holding a small, old, dusty book and examining it carefully. To Axel the book looks boring. But the Professor's very excited.

He explains that it's written by hand, in runes—mysterious Viking letters, from Iceland.

As the Professor talks, a piece of parchment [1] falls out of the book. He unfolds it eagerly. He can see that it's not as old as the book, though still written in runes.

But, to his amazement, he can't work out what they mean! The runes are jumbled up, then arranged in groups of seven. But why?

Martha opens the door to say that lunch is ready. She's made some nice soup, then there's eggs and meat . . . The Professor interrupts her angrily.

Professor Lidenbrock stays in his study, puzzling over the runes. But Axel is very hungry. He goes downstairs and eats two lunches— his own, and the Professor's.

1. parchment: sheepskin, specially prepared for writing on.

There's a secret to it...

Just as Axel is finishing his meal, he hears the Professor shouting and hurries to the study. The Professor is sure that the runes must be in some kind of code . . .

. . . and he needs Axel's help to decipher it. As he reads out each code word, Axel must write it down. With luck, they'll discover a clue to the mystery.

But all they get is a list of nonsense words. How can they make any sense of them?

Arne Saknussemm!

The Professor thinks he knows. He searches through the book for a clue that will break the code. He thinks he's found it—the name of an ancient Icelandic alchemist[1] who once owned the book—and wrote the parchment.

Arne Saknussemm lived centuries ago—around 1550. He tried all sorts of weird experiments, and took part in exciting explorations. He wanted to find out more about the Earth—just like the Professor himself.

Avicenna (Ibn Sina)
980–1037

Lully
(Ramón Llull)
c.1235–1315

Francis Bacon
1561–1626

Paracelsus
1493–1541

Nor will you, Axel!

Axel listens as the Professor lists many other great scientists from history. They all made amazing discoveries. This parchment probably records something discovered by Saknussemm.

Wildly, the Professor declares that he won't eat or sleep until he's found out about Saknussemm's discovery.

1. alchemist: something between a scientist and a magician.

AXEL CRACKS THE CODE

Axel and the Professor study the message in runes one more time. They think it may be written in Latin.

While the Professor talks on, Axel grows drowsy. He cannot help daydreaming. He thinks of Gräuben . . .

She's so nice, so clever, and so pretty! Axel wants to marry her. Gräuben loves him, too; secretly they're engaged. Now, Gräuben's away on a visit, and Axel misses her.

Wham! Crash! Axel wakes up with a start as the Professor thumps his fist down on the table. He's had an idea!

To test his theory, the Professor asks Axel to write down the first sentence he can think of. Axel must arrange the letters like the runes on the parchment.

Half-dreaming, Axel writes, "I love you very much, my dear little Gräuben." When he reads this, the Professor's very startled at first. But he doesn't really mind. In any case, he's much more interested in deciphering the message.

The Professor tries again. He asks Axel to write down the letters of the mysterious parchment, but this time in a different arrangement. Axel does as he is told—but the words are still nonsense.

We shall have to starve!

Baffled, the Professor shrieks and rushes out of the door.

Downstairs in her kitchen, Martha is still worrying.

Axel wonders whether he should run after the Professor. Or should he go and find Gräuben? She's kind and sensible—she'll know what to do.

What can it possibly mean?

Oh no!

He decides he'd better stay at home and wait for the Professor to return. He sits down in a comfy armchair and thinks again and again about the secret message.

Idly, he flicks his Latin translation of the message from side to side. As the paper flashes to and fro, he finds he can read it. At last he understands—the message is written backwards!

He paces up and down the room to calm himself. The message is clear— and it's terrifying!

Axel reads the message again, but there's no mistake. It can only mean one thing. Axel thinks, "The Professor must never hear of this!" and decides to burn the parchment.

At that same moment, the Professor walks in. He's calmer now, and more reasonable. He's got yet another new idea to try out. He hurries to his desk and starts making calculations.

THE PARCHMENT DECIPHERED

Are you going to have any supper?

I will not speak!

Axel says nothing. He just watches as the Professor struggles for hours with pages and pages of numbers.

Martha tells them that food is ready, but the Professor ignores her— and Axel has to go hungry, too.

By now, Axel is worried. He doesn't know what to do. He knows the calculations won't decipher the code. But he's frightened to say that he's already done so.

They sit in the study all night. The Professor works, while Axel dozes. In the morning, Martha asks for permission to leave the house to shop for food, but the Professor won't let her go.

Uncle . . .

Aha!

By the afternoon, Axel's very hungry. And he's worried about Martha. It's not fair to make her starve. She's getting old, and works hard to look after them all. He decides to speak . . .

With a sigh, Axel tells the Professor that he can understand the mysterious message. His uncle roars with delight—then demands to know what it means. Fearfully, Axel reads: "Descend into the crater of Sneffels . . . and you will reach the center of the Earth."

The Professor jumps with joy, then rushes to speak to Martha immediately.

They have a quick meal, then the Professor takes Axel back to the study. He tells him to pack their bags for a long journey.

Axel protests. There can't be many others who'd dare make such a dangerous journey. Does the Professor really plan to go to the center of the Earth?

In reply, the Professor asks Axel to bring a fine atlas from the bookshelves. Together they look at maps showing Iceland and its volcanoes. The Professor points out the one called Sneffels.

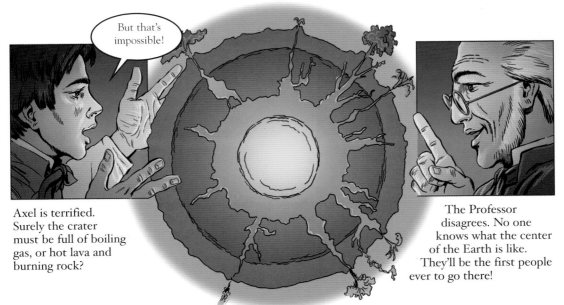

Axel is terrified. Surely the crater must be full of boiling gas, or hot lava and burning rock?

The Professor disagrees. No one knows what the center of the Earth is like. They'll be the first people ever to go there!

13

GRÄUBEN SAYS "GO!"

Axel is overwhelmed by the Professor's enthusiasm, but he's still very scared. He leaves the study in a daze, and sets off by himself for a long walk.

He needs to think. And the more he thinks, the more worried he becomes. But then he meets Gräuben . . .

Gräuben will help him! She knows the Professor. She'll understand, and advise. Gräuben listens carefully as Axel describes the mysterious message and its translation. Then she speaks—and her words astonish Axel even more.

Gräuben says "Go!" An adventure like this will make a great start for Axel's career. He can show that he's brave, strong, and clever. She wishes she could go too. But she'll wait, and when Axel returns, she'll marry him.

By the time they reach home, it's getting dark. They were expecting the house to be peaceful—but the front porch is full of travelling gear, and the Professor is waiting to greet them. Axel feels exhausted already.

The Professor tells Axel to hurry up and get ready, because they're leaving the day after tomorrow.

Next morning, Gräuben helps Axel pack all he needs for the journey. She's calm and quiet, but Axel's still feeling frightened. It seems that he has no choice.

Is the Master out of his mind?

Martha shares Axel's fears. She can't believe that he and the Professor really are heading for the center of the Earth.

That night—his last in Hamburg—Axel sleeps very badly. He dreams he's falling into a bottomless pit.

Gräuben!

When he wakes up, he's terrified.

Go, Axel dear, go!

At breakfast, Axel can't eat a thing, but the Professor seems very cheerful. They load their baggage onto the cart and head for the railway station. This is the start of their adventure! Gräuben and Martha can't help crying as they wave good-bye.

TO ICELAND!

They board an express train to rush them to Denmark. There, they plan to catch the first boat heading for Iceland. There's no time to lose. According to the parchment, they must reach Sneffels, the volcano, before Midsummer's Day.

As they arrive in Copenhagen, Denmark's capital, Axel still thinks that the Professor's plans are mad.

Come aboard on Tuesday.

First they visit the Museum of Antiquities. The Director, Professor Thomson, welcomes them, and Professor Lidenbrock asks him lots of questions. He also asks for help to find a ship sailing to Iceland.

They go to the docks, where the Director introduces them to a ship's master, Captain Bjarne. The Captain's ship, the *Valkyrie*, will soon be setting sail. It carries cargo to Reykjavik, the capital of Iceland.

I can't do it!

The Professor's very pleased. "Things are going very well indeed!" he says. And, while they're waiting for the ship, Axel has time to do some sightseeing.

The Director gives Professor Lidenbrock a letter of introduction to the Danish Governor of Iceland.[1]

To help Axel conquer his fear of heights and deep, dark spaces, they visit a church with a tall spire. The Professor makes Axel climb to the top and look down, over and over again, until he stops feeling dizzy.

1. Governor of Iceland: Iceland was ruled by Denmark at this time.

June 2nd, 1863

Sneffels! Sneffels!

At last it's time to go. The *Valkyrie* glides out of the harbor. But the weather soon gets rough, and the Professor becomes seasick. He stays in his cabin until they reach Iceland.

On shore, they are met by Baron Trampe, the Governor of Iceland. He's surprised to see visitors, but the Professor shows him the letter from the Museum in Copenhagen.

It asks the Icelanders to help the two German scientists. The Mayor of Reykjavik, Mr. Finsen, agrees to help.

He takes them to meet the head science teacher at Reykjavik School, Mr. Fridriksson. They stay with the teacher's family.

The kind teacher tries to answer all the Professor's questions. While they're busy, Axel goes outside to explore. The Reykjavik houses are small and plain, but the people look strong and healthy.

?!

The Professor wants to find out more about the alchemist Arne Saknussemm—but the shelves at Iceland's National Library are half empty!

Mr. Fridriksson explains that Icelanders love studying, and have borrowed many of the books to read at home.

Excellent! Splendid!

The Professor asks where else he might find books written by Saknussemm. "Nowhere," says the teacher—they were all burned long ago. So Saknussemm's discoveries are still secret!

HANS THE HUNTER

It's time to leave Reykjavik and head for Sneffels, the volcano. Mr. Fridriksson has found them a guide, Hans the Hunter.

Hans tells them that he usually hunts eider ducks for their feathers. But he's willing to go anywhere with them, as long as they pay him at the end of each week.

Yet again they must pack all they need for their journey. But now they take only food, medicine, a gun, some gold, and the Professor's scientific instruments.

Et quacumque viam dederit fortuna sequamur.[1]

The schoolteacher gives them a map, showing the rocks and minerals in the ground and the best route for their journey.

Leaving Reykjavik

Good horse! Good horse!

They travel on ponies through wild country: along the coast, up mountain slopes, past barren rocks, through bogs, and across bleak, windswept moors. At first Axel thinks it's fun—just like going on vacation.

Saellvertu![2]

But by evening he's tired out. He's delighted when they stop to eat and stay the night with a welcoming farmer's family.

1. Et quacumque viam dederit fortuna sequamur: And let us go where fortune leads us. (Latin)
2. Saellvertu!: Be happy!

The next day, the country grows wilder, harsher, and more threatening. There are no trees, few animals, and no cozy farms. They shelter in a drafty hovel, where Axel dreams of monsters.

Getting close to Sneffels

So this is the giant[1] I am going to defeat!

The village of Stapi

They plan to stay with a church minister and his wife. But the minister is very poor, and the house is not very comfortable. They decide not to stay and rest, but hurry on to Sneffels.

They leave the ponies, but Hans hires three strong porters to carry their baggage. They'll climb together to the summit of Sneffels, but then the porters will leave them. For the rest of their journey to the center of the Earth, they'll be on their own.

1. the giant: Sneffels, the volcano.

INTO THE VOLCANO

June 22nd, 1863

Axel is worried that Sneffels will erupt. Even though it's stayed quiet since 1229, he still has nightmares about exploding volcanoes.

We have nothing to fear.

The Professor reassures him; the volcano's steaming gently. They'll only need to worry if the steam blasts out fiercely, or if the earth shakes, or if they hear rumblings.

They climb onward and upward toward Sneffels' twin peaks that tower almost 5,000 feet into the sky. They pass streams of ash and columns of cooled, solid lava, thrown up by past eruptions.

The sight makes Axel think again about the Earth, and how it was formed, long ago. What made volcanoes rise? Why was lava runny? He feels sure that the Earth must still be hot inside—and that to want to go there is absolute madness.

They climb higher, through snow. Then Hans shouts an urgent warning. He's seen a mistour—a mountain whirlwind—approaching.

They run for their lives as the whirlwind comes close. At last they reach the far side of the mountain. The whirlwind roars around, but they're out of its path. They've survived! They're safe—for the moment.

They reach Scartaris, the peak on Sneffels that Saknussemm described in the secret message. It's very late, and by now they're exhausted!

The next morning they gaze at wonderful sights. Even Axel admires them. There's a crater on the peak; they lean over its rim and peer deep down inside.

They scramble to the bottom and find three huge vents,[2] like pipes leading far underground. But which one should they follow?

They don't know—until the Professor finds a stone pillar carved with the name of Arne Saknussemm. According to the parchment, the shadow of the pillar will show them the way.

1. Hastigt! Hastigt!: Hurry! Hurry!
2. vents: tunnels made by lava and gas escaping from the volcano.

INTO THE UNKNOWN

June 28th, 1863

Be careful!

They wait for three long days until Saknussemm's stone casts a shadow on the middle vent. They climb down it, using rope, while rocks fall all around them.

It's scary and dangerous, but the Professor still manages to make scientific observations. After ten hours they reach the bottom. Once they have eaten, they fall asleep, utterly exhausted.

The next day, Axel calculates they've descended 2,800 feet. The Professor reckons they're at sea level now, just like their home town of Hamburg.

Now our journey begins!

They're in a dark, rocky chamber with a tunnel leading off. Holding electric torches—the very latest technology—they enter the tunnel. They march downward, heading south and east. Even Axel notices how beautiful the rocks are.

It's magnificent!

It's getting hotter the deeper they go. They're now 10,000 feet below sea level. Axel is rather puzzled that it's not boiling hot—but pleased to still be alive!

By evening it's time to rest again. They eat and drink hungrily. But Axel has another worry: they're running short of water.

Now another problem: the tunnel splits in two. Which path should they take? There's no way to tell. The Professor chooses the eastern one. It leads through magnificent natural pillars of rock . . .

A coal mine!

. . . then to rocks full of wonderful fossils. Axel says that this means they're heading up, not down[1]— but the Professor won't listen.

By now, their water bottles are nearly empty. The Professor says they must ration their drinking: just a few sips each, every day.

Axel can't sleep, he's so thirsty. He worries that he'll die here—and never see Gräuben again.

After three days the tunnel opens out into a vast underground cavern. It's fantastic—but it doesn't have any water for drinking, and Axel's feeling desperate.

Grimly, they walk on for another day. But then they can't go any further. It's a dead end. They're stuck! And they still don't have any water.

1. up, not down: because fossils are only found in young rocks, close to the surface.

WATER, WATER!

The Professor is brave. Hans is calm. Axel complains bitterly. All they have to drink is gin, which burns his throat.

Each day they feel weaker, until they can hardly walk. Each step brings agony. But they stagger back along the way they came . . .

. . . until Axel collapses, unconscious. The Professor gives him their precious last few drops of water. He's been saving it for emergencies.

Poor child!

We must go back.

Axel feels better. But he wants to go back to the surface, while he's still strong enough to survive.

Master!

Axel asks Hans to go with him, but Hans refuses. He's promised to work for the Professor, and will stay loyal to the end.

And the Professor won't give in. He has a new suggestion to make: why don't they try the western fork of the tunnel? It seems promising. Axel is horrified.

Now we are on the right track!

Slowly, they set off. Hans, being the strongest, leads the way. The Professor's pleased to find ancient rocks. This makes him think that they are heading downward again.

But Axel's too weak to walk further. Sad and angry, the Professor fears they'll have to return to the surface after all. But Hans goes exploring.

Drowsily, Axel sees Hans wander away, then come back quickly. He's saying something excitedly in his own language.

Hans is right! They can all hear rushing water. Hans smashes at the rocks with a pickaxe—and clouds of steam gush through. The water is boiling!

They wait for the steam to cool back to water, then drink it thirstily. Hans is a hero! He's saved their lives—and made sure their expedition can continue.

As they relax, refreshed, the Professor has a clever idea. All water flows downward, so if they follow it, they can't fail to find the center of the Earth!

1. Vatten!: Water!

LOST IN THE DARK

July 9th, 1863

For two days they follow the water as it flows down a gently sloping tunnel. Axel's feeling better now, and enjoying the adventure. But then the water suddenly disappears into a deep, dark crevasse. Where it goes they must follow!

Under the sea!

Each day the Professor makes careful scientific measurements. He's says they're no longer under Iceland. Instead, there are whales and ships directly overhead!

They rope themselves together and clamber down a twisting staircase of natural rock. They descend for 48 hours. Now they're 13 miles underground.

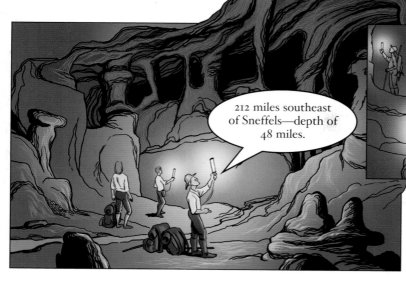

212 miles southeast of Sneffels—depth of 48 miles.

After four more days they reach a gigantic grotto. The Professor says they'll rest here while he makes more scientific studies. They've spent 20 days underground.

Feeling better, Axel hurries on ahead. When he turns around, he's alone. The stream has gone. He's lost!

Axel falls to his knees and prays. He decides he must walk uphill, to try to get back to the crater.

He stumbles on for a while, but then the tunnel ends. His torch flickers and dies. He's in total darkness now—completely lost and alone.

Axel thinks he's doomed to a horrible, lingering death, alone in the dark, 75 miles underground. He runs around wildly, then collapses, exhausted.

UNDERGROUND SEA

Axel lies unconscious for hours. When he wakes up he's weak and dizzy. He's about to faint again, when he hears a noise like thunder.

He listens again. Surely those are voices? But where are they coming from? They must be bouncing off the rocks, like an echo. He shouts as loud as he can . . .

. . . and hears the Professor shouting back at him! The Professor explains that they've been searching for him and firing their guns as signals.

Together, they use watches to measure the speed of their words travelling through the rock. They're 3½ miles apart. It's a long way!

The Professor tells Axel to be brave and head downhill. Before long they'll be reunited. But Axel trips, and finds himself falling.

He wakes up, wrapped in blankets. He feels weak and bruised all over, but at least he's no longer alone—Hans and the Professor are watching over him.

August 10th, 1863

Human words are totally inadequate . . .

Axel sees waves, clouds, cliffs, and a strange light in the sky.

Astonishing, magnificent, splendid!

A forest of giant mushrooms grows on the shore.

They see massive dinosaur bones and prehistoric trees.

Look, Axel, and admire it all!

By the next day, Axel feels better. And all around he sees wonders. But where did these strange things come from? What further marvels—and terrors—lie ahead?

MONSTERS OF THE DEEP

August 12th, 1863

"We are 900 feet from Iceland."

Hans can't wait to get to the far side of that amazing sea. Axel and the Professor watch while he builds a raft out of fossil wood.

The next morning they set sail. The sea is calm but eerie. Their raft is surrounded by giant seaweed, each frond over 3,000 feet long.

"This fish has long been extinct."

"What a dream this is! Where is it taking me?"

Axel daydreams about other prehistoric creatures.

Hans tries fishing but doesn't get a bite for hours. At last he hooks a fish and hauls it on board. It's blind—and prehistoric!

"Tänder![1]"

They sail on and on. There's still no sign of land. Axel worries: are live prehistoric beasts lurking nearby, ready to attack?

Hans lowers a big hook deep down into the sea. When he pulls it up, there are deep marks on it—made by giant jaws!

1. Tänder: Teeth.

Yes, there are monsters below! And they are fighting! The little raft is tossed about helplessly as the fearsome sea giants splash and dive.

Axel and the Professor watch, awestruck, as the sea creatures fight furiously. Will they be attacked next? Or will the raft be capsized?

At last, one of the monsters is fatally wounded.

They sail on and on. Will they be lost forever on this vast inland sea? Hans hears a strange noise. It's a jet of water, 500 feet high.

It's a killer blast of superheated water from deep underground. They sail past safely, but what's that ahead? A storm is about to break over their fragile raft.

1. geysir: geyser, waterspout (Icelandic).

SHIPWRECKED!

August 21st, 1863

Let the wind seize us!

We are done for!

Where are we going?

Now we can start travelling by land again.

The storm rages for three days. They are battered, bruised, and exhausted. A bolt of lightning glows, sparks, and fizzes—then suddenly all is dark.

At last the wind drops and the sea is calm. The raft crashes against rocks in shallow water, and they wade ashore. Wet, cold, tired, but thankful, they shelter on the beach.

Uncle . . . what about our return journey?

You are thinking about the return journey . . .

. . . before we have even arrived?

Axel no longer wants to go on toward the center of the Earth. He'd rather be at home with Gräuben. The Professor assures him that they will get home one way or another.

While they talk, Hans has made a good job of rescuing their belongings from the shipwrecked raft and repairing it.

Their compass looks undamaged, but it tells them that what they thought was south is really north!

The Professor is very puzzled. But at last he thinks he understands. Their raft must have changed direction during the storm. They've been sailing backward!

The Professor says there's only one thing they can do, set sail and cross the dangerous sea once again. Axel is horrified but can't change the Professor's mind.

On shore, they find mountains of huge, dry, gleaming bones—the remains of massive prehistoric animals. Then, all of a sudden, the Professor shouts out loud, his voice trembling with excitement.

The head belongs to a man who died long ago. The Professor is fascinated. But Axel has an alarming thought. If sea monsters still live here underground—so might wild, prehistoric humans!

THE GIANT AND THE DAGGER

August 26th, 1863

Mastodons! Giant living prehistoric elephants!

Axel and the Professor walk on, exploring, through a forest of the living dead. All around them are trees that became extinct on the Earth's surface many thousands of years earlier. Suddenly, Axel hears noises.

Oh, no—a giant, living prehistoric man, almost 13 feet tall!

Come on! Come on!

They run for their lives, back toward the shore. Will the giant follow them? Will he attack?

Somebody has been here before us!

No—the giant stays under his tree. Back by their raft, in safety, Axel spies something shiny in the sand.

A sixteenth-century weapon!

It's a dagger. The blade is twisted at the tip—it's been used to carve a message in the rock.

Sure enough, someone has carved initials next to a tunnel. They're faint, but still readable.

Arne Saknussemm was here, hundreds of years ago. This must be the way toward the center of the Earth! But the tunnel is blocked by an enormous boulder.

The Professor decides they must blast their way through the rock with guncotton.[1] Axel gets the fuse ready. Then they wait overnight, ready to set off the explosion.

At dawn, Axel lights the fuse and dashes out of the tunnel. He climbs onto the raft, and they push off quickly, out to sea.

There's a blinding flash, a mighty crash, and a deafening roar and rumble. The rocks shatter, revealing a vast, dark abyss.[2] The sea pours into the opening, and the raft carrying Axel, the Professor, and Hans is swept along with it.

1. guncotton: a kind of high explosive.
2. abyss: deep hole, with no sight of the bottom.

BOILED ALIVE?

August 27th, 1863

They fall for an hour or more, clinging to the raft with all their strength. At last they reach the bottom of the abyss, and the roar of the water stops. They find that they're at the bottom of a narrow shaft—and the water level is rising.

The Professor's right. As the water flows into the abyss, it's lifting them upward. Axel wonders what will happen if the shaft has no opening at the top. It might end in a cave, or a wall of rock!

It's a miserable thought. The Professor suggests they have a meal to cheer themselves up. But—more bad news—almost all their food has been washed overboard. Soon they'll be starving.

As the water keeps rising, they begin to feel hotter and hotter. Axel peers over the edge of the raft.

He's puzzled—surely it should get cooler as they rise toward the Earth's surface? But the Professor's not worried at all.

They hear loud rumblings all around. The rocks crack and shudder. Weird flames flicker among clouds of choking gas, and hot lava swirls toward them.

At last, Axel understands. An underground volcano is erupting. Now he's even more terrified—they'll all be blown to bits by the explosion!

August 29th, 1863

Miraculously, they're still alive—they've survived the volcanic explosion. The eruption has blasted them back to the surface of the Earth, onto a steep, rocky hillside.

Their compass shows that they've been travelling north, but this is clearly not Iceland! It's hot and sunny. Down below, the sea's bright blue. There are fruit trees and grapevines growing.

Behind them the volcano is still gurgling and rumbling, so they hurry downhill for safety. As they run, they meet a boy from a nearby farm. He's scared at first by their wild appearance.

The farm boy is the first normal living creature they've seen since they went underground weeks ago. He tells them the name of the volcano. They are in Sicily[1]—the compass was affected by the bolt of lightning, and they have been travelling south instead of north!

Sicily is a beautiful place, warm, fertile, welcoming. As they walk toward the nearest town, they munch fruit and drink spring water. Both are delicious!

1. Sicily: an island off the south coast of Italy.

September 9th, 1863

They've survived, safe and sound, after many extraordinary adventures! Axel's delighted, the Professor's relieved, and even the calm, quiet Hans is smiling. At the town, kind fishermen give them food and let them rest until they feel stronger. Then it's time to start travelling again.

This time they're heading home. They'll sail by boat from Sicily to the south of France, then take the train across Germany.

Our journey began . . .

At last they reach Hamburg and hurry to the Professor's house. Martha and Gräuben are overjoyed to see them. Everyone wants to hear their story. The Professor is a celebrity!

Färval![1]

Now you need never leave me again!

But Hans can't wait to go home to Iceland. With many thanks, Axel and the Professor bid him good-bye. They would not have survived their adventures without him.

Axel and Gräuben finally marry, as they had hoped all along. They continue to live happily in the Professor's house in Hamburg. The Professor's happy too, because his adventures have made him more famous than ever.

The End

1. Färval: Farewell.

JULES VERNE (1828–1905)

Jules Verne was born in 1828, in Nantes, northwest France. His father was a successful lawyer, and the family was wealthy. Nantes was a busy seaport, and young Jules loved to watch the sailing ships in the harbor and daydream about their exciting ocean voyages.

At nine years old, Jules was sent to a boarding school, along with his favorite brother, Paul. Jules was a clever child and enjoyed lessons. He studied French, Latin, math, science, literature, and philosophy.

Jules Verne, photographed by Nadar.

PARIS

Although Jules's father liked to write poems in his spare time, he did not think writing was a suitable way to earn a living. So, when Jules left school in 1847, his father sent him to Paris to study law. For ten years, Jules pretended to be studying—but in fact he was practicing his writer's skills by creating plays for the theater (which were not particularly successful). He lived in cheap lodgings and met actors, dancers, painters, and well-known writers such as Alexandre Dumas, author of the popular romantic adventure story *The Three Musketeers*. Dumas encouraged Jules and offered him good advice.

LOVE AND MARRIAGE

In 1856, when Jules was 28, he met Honorine de Viane, a widow with two young daughters. They fell in love, married, and remained devoted partners all their lives. They had one son, Michel. Honorine admired Jules's writing and encouraged him to continue. But, to support his family, he worked as a stockbroker, helping investors to buy and sell shares in businesses. He made money, but found the work much less interesting than writing.

A CHANGE OF DIRECTION

Around the same time, Jules Verne met a Parisian publisher, Pierre-Jules Hetzel, who published the works of some of the best-known French writers of that time. Hetzel thought Jules's work was fresh, original, different—but often rather gloomy and depressing. So he asked Jules to make changes to the text. He wanted more comedy, less politics, and happy endings. Jules agreed to try. His new books were a success, and the two men remained friends and colleagues for many years.

A BUSY CAREER

Jules Verne worked hard and wrote very quickly. His first adventure story, *Five Weeks in a Balloon*, was published in 1863. (*Journey to the Center of the Earth* was his third.) Between 1863 and 1905, Verne completed at least two books every year—an astonishing total of 20 short stories, 30 plays, and 65 full-length novels. He also read a great deal, mostly about science and geography, and interviewed scientists and inventors. His books were based on detailed research and featured many of the latest ideas and discoveries of his time.

As well as stories, Verne also wrote short articles on geography and songs for operas. He wrote in French, his native tongue, but most of his writings were soon translated into English, German, and many other languages. His best-loved story, *Around the World in Eighty Days*, was made into a play and performed in French theaters for years. Many others were published in weekly installments in newspapers and magazines.

FAME AND FORTUNE

Sales of his books and plays made Jules a rich man. He bought a fine house and a beautiful yacht, the *Saint-Michel*. Although he wrote some of the world's most famous adventure stories, Jules was not a great traveller—but he did enjoy sailing around Europe on his vacations. In 1867 he travelled to the USA with his brother Paul, visiting natural wonders such as Niagara Falls.

In 1870 the French government gave Jules its top award for his achievements: membership of the Légion d'Honneur (Fellowship of Honor). He was happy, wealthy, famous—and then a strange and sad thing happened. In 1886 Jules was shot in the leg by his nephew Gaston, and for the rest of his life he walked with a painful limp. But this did not stop him from writing. In 1888, he began to take an active part in local politics and was elected as a town councillor.

Jules Verne continued to produce new books right up until his death in 1905, at age 77. As a sign of respect, many streets and public buildings in France were renamed after him. Today, over 100 years after Jules Verne died, he is still one of the most widely read authors in the world.

French postage stamp with a portrait of Jules Verne and a scene from his novel Twenty Thousand Leagues Under the Sea.

MAP OF THE JOURNEY

APPROXIMATE ROUTE TAKEN BY AXEL AND THE PROFESSOR

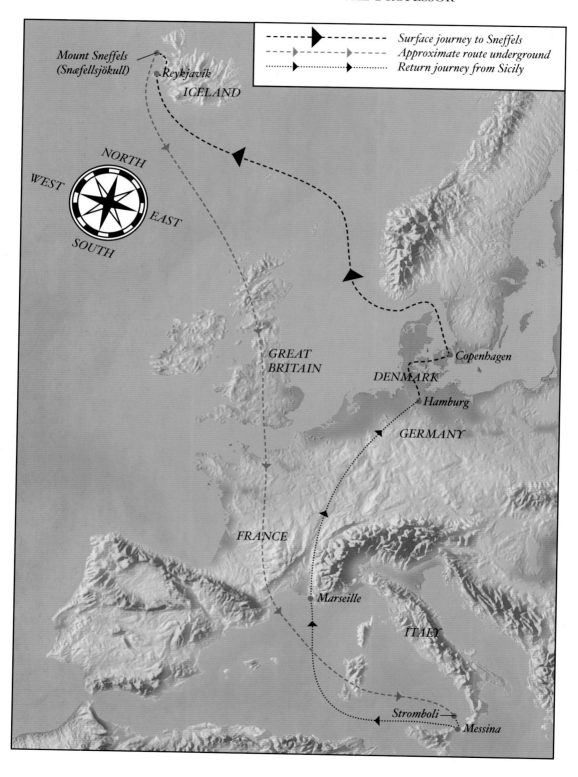

––––▶––––	Surface journey to Sneffels
––––▶––––	Approximate route underground
·····▶·····	Return journey from Sicily

Mount Sneffels
(Snæfellsjökull)

Reykjavik

ICELAND

NORTH

WEST

EAST

SOUTH

GREAT
BRITAIN

Copenhagen

DENMARK

Hamburg

GERMANY

FRANCE

Marseille

ITALY

Stromboli

Messina

FACT AND FICTION

Jules Verne lived at a time of fast technological change and great scientific discoveries. He used many new inventions—such as submarines and hot-air balloons—to inspire his stories and made use of new discoveries such as fossils and electromagnetism.

Verne joined nineteenth-century scientists in puzzling about unsolved mysteries: What was the Earth made of? Were there really monsters lurking deep in the oceans? Would people ever be able to travel in space? He also joined in one of the latest scientific debates: how does change happen? Is it caused by slow evolution (as suggested by British scientist Charles Darwin in 1859) or by dramatic catastrophes?

In *Journey to the Center of the Earth*, Jules Verne explores several popular theories about how the Earth was formed. At the time the book was published, in 1864, some scholars still thought that the Earth might be hollow, with lots of smaller, empty spheres inside—a belief which had been held for a long time. But nineteenth-century geologists, who studied ancient rocks, suggested that many had been laid down gradually, over millions of years, and that in this case the Earth must be solid.

Verne also discusses what causes natural disasters such as earthquakes, volcanic eruptions, and mass extinctions of species. He mentions fossils, prehistoric people, how coal was formed, and the theory of human evolution.

INSIDE THE EARTH

Scientists now know that the Earth is made up of three parts: the outer crust, the mantle, and the core.

• The **crust** is a thin layer of solid rock, about 25 miles deep under dry land, but only 4 miles deep under the oceans.
• The **mantle** lies below the crust and is about 1,800 miles deep. It is made of hot rock—between 1,600 and 5,400°F—that moves very slowly.
• The **core** of the Earth measures about 4,000 miles in diameter. Its outer rim is solid, but its center is mostly made of very hot molten (melted) iron. There may be a solid, compressed section right in the middle.

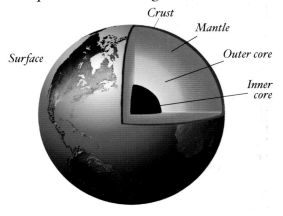

Crust
Mantle
Surface
Outer core
Inner core

This is what most scientists today think the inside of the Earth is like.

The deepest man-sized holes made in the Earth's crust so far are diamond mines in South Africa, which descend for 2 miles. The heat and pressure there are so intense that miners can dig no deeper—so in real life a journey to the center of the Earth is just not possible.

SCIENCE AND TECHNOLOGY

IN JULES VERNE'S LIFETIME

1828
Hot blast furnace for mass-producing cast iron invented by James Neilson, Scotland.

1829
Alphabet of raised dots, for blind people to read, designed by Louis Braille, France.
Steam locomotive *Rocket* built by George Stephenson, England.

1831
Steam-powered buses in London, England.

1831–1833
Major discoveries in electricity and magnetism by Michael Faraday, England.

1832
Mechanical computer, called a "difference engine," invented by Charles Babbage, England.
Streetcars introduced in New York, USA.

1834
Mechanical grain-harvesting machine invented by Cyrus McCormick, USA.

1835
First photographic negatives, by William Henry Fox Talbot, England.
Screw propeller for ships invented by John Ericsson, Sweden, and Francis Smith, USA.
Revolver invented by Samuel Colt, USA.

1836
British biologist Charles Darwin completes around-the-world voyage in HMS *Beagle* to investigate wildlife in its environment.

1837
Regular crossings of the Atlantic by Isambard Kingdom Brunel's steamship *Great Western*.

1839
First national postal system set up in UK by Sir Rowland Hill.

1841
Word "dinosaur" invented by British archaeologist Richard Owen.

1843
First tunnel under the River Thames in London, England, by French engineer Marc Brunel.

1844–1846
Anesthetics (medicines to ease pain and cause unconsciousness) pioneered in USA.

1845
First spiral galaxy discovered by William Parsons, Ireland.
Pneumatic (air-filled) tire invented by Robert Thomson, Scotland.
British scientist John Snow proves that polluted water is the cause of mass-killer disease cholera.

1846
Neptune identified by Johann Galle, Germany.

1848
Diving bell invented by James Eads, USA.

1851
Undersea telegraph cable laid between England and France.
Refrigerator invented by John Gorrie, USA.
Iron and glass Crystal Palace designed by Sir Joseph Paxton to house the Great Exhibition of modern technology in London, England.

1852
First steam-powered airship flight by Henri Giffard, France.

1853
First people-carrying glider built by George Cayley, England.

1855
Converter (furnace for making steel) invented by Henry Bessemer, England.

1856
Remains of prehistoric Neanderthal man found by Pierre Broca, France.
First photographs from the air, by Nadar, France.

1857
Steam plough invented by John Fowler, England.

1858
First iron passenger liner, *Great Britain*, built by Isambard Kingdom Brunel, England.

1859
Charles Darwin suggests theories of natural selection ("survival of the fittest") and evolution.
First oil-drilling rig, USA.

1861
Color photography demonstrated by Scottish physicist James Clerk Maxwell.

1862
Machine gun invented by Richard Gatling, USA.

1863
Antiseptic (clean environment) surgery pioneered by Joseph Lister, England.
First underground railway opened in London, England.

1865
Major discoveries in heredity and genetics by Gregor Mendel, Moravia.
Louis Pasteur, France, discovers that bacteria cause disease.

1867
Dynamite invented by Alfred Nobel, Sweden.

1868
Fossils of Cro-Magnon people—the earliest in Europe—discovered by Edouard Lartet, France.

1873
Major advance in understanding light energy by James Clerk Maxwell, Scotland.

1876
Four-stroke internal-combustion engine invented by Nikolaus Otto, Germany.
Telephone invented by Alexander Graham Bell, Scotland/USA.
Mass-produced canned foods on sale in the USA.
First refrigerated ships transport meat and other perishable goods around the world.

1877
Major advance in understanding sound by British scientist Lord Rayleigh.

1878
Microphone invented by Emil Berliner, Germany/USA.

1879
Electric lightbulb invented by Thomas Edison, USA, and Joseph Swann, England.

1883
First electric trams in London, England.
First high-speed motorboat built by Gottlieb Daimler, Germany.

1885
First reliable motorbike built by Gottlieb Daimler and Karl Benz, Germany. They also invent a petrol engine.

1886
Four-wheeled, petrol-driven motor car made by Daimler, Germany.

Water closet (flush lavatory) invented by Thomas Crapper, England.

1887
Gramophone invented by Emil Berliner, Germany/USA.

1889
Milky Way photographed by E. E. Barnard, USA.
Eiffel Tower built in Paris, France.

1892
Zipper invented by Whitcombe Judson, USA.
Diesel engine invented by Rudolf Diesel, Germany.

1894
Major advance in understanding radio waves by Oliver Lodge, England.

1895
X-rays discovered by Wilhelm Röntgen, Germany.
First motion pictures produced by Auguste and Louis Lumière, France.

1896–1898
Radioactivity discovered by Henri Becquerel, France, and Marie Curie, Poland/France.

1897
Cathode-ray tube, later used in television, invented by Karl Braun, Germany.
Hydrofoil built by Comte de Lambert, France.

1898
First modern submarine invented by John Holland, Ireland/USA.

1900
First hydrogen-filled airship designed by Graf Zeppelin, Germany.

1901
Guglielmo Marconi, Italy, sends telegrams by radio waves.

1903
First airplane flight, by Orville and Wilbur Wright, USA.
High-powered rockets invented by Konstantin Tsiolkovsky, Russia.

1905
Albert Einstein (Germany/USA) publishes his revolutionary Special Theory of Relativity.

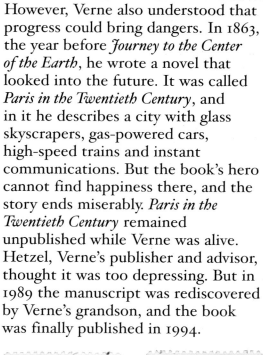

Jules Verne has often been called "the father of science fiction." He did not really set out to invent a whole new type of fiction, but he was one of the first writers to realize that scientific ideas or unsolved questions could be the inspiration for exciting, adventurous entertainments.

Like many other people living at the time, Verne greatly admired the scientists and engineers of his day. He was interested in their experiments and amazed by their achievements (just a few of which are listed on pages 44–45). He saw that many of these new inventions and discoveries could be used to improve people's lives and offer them wonderful new opportunities.

However, Verne also understood that progress could bring dangers. In 1863, the year before *Journey to the Center of the Earth*, he wrote a novel that looked into the future. It was called *Paris in the Twentieth Century*, and in it he describes a city with glass skyscrapers, gas-powered cars, high-speed trains and instant communications. But the book's hero cannot find happiness there, and the story ends miserably. *Paris in the Twentieth Century* remained unpublished while Verne was alive. Hetzel, Verne's publisher and advisor, thought it was too depressing. But in 1989 the manuscript was rediscovered by Verne's grandson, and the book was finally published in 1994.

Postage stamps commemorating Verne's novels.

OTHER BOOKS BY JULES VERNE

Here are the English titles of some of Verne's most famous works:

1863 – *Five Weeks in a Balloon*
1864 – *The English at the North Pole*
1864 – *Journey to the Center of the Earth*
1865 – *From the Earth to the Moon*
1869–1870 – *Twenty Thousand Leagues Under the Sea*

1871 – *A Floating City*
1873 – *Around the World in Eighty Days*
1874 – *The Mysterious Island*
1886 – *The Clipper of the Clouds*
1904 – *Master of the World*
1905 – *Lighthouse at the End of the World*

BASED ON *JOURNEY TO THE CENTER OF THE EARTH*

Many films and TV programs have been made about journeys deep into the Earth. Here are some of the best-known. Most have been inspired by Jules Verne's story, and some have the same title as his book—but most of them made big changes to Verne's original characters and plot.

1909 Silent film, now lost, France.

1951 *Unknown World*, USA.
Scientists hide underground to escape a nuclear explosion. Only loosely inspired by Verne's story.

1959 Hollywood spectacular, USA.
Starring James Mason and Pat Boone. Fairly close to Verne's story, but also featuring an evil nobleman, said to be descended from Arne Saknussemm, and live lizards dressed as dinosaurs.

1976 *The Fabulous Journey to the Center of the Earth*, Spain.
Feature film starring Kenneth More.

1977 Cartoon version, Australia.
By famous cartoon artist Richard Slapczynski. Follows some strands of Verne's story, but introduces a dinosaur egg, which is brought to the surface and hatched.

1993 Film made for TV, USA.
An underground expedition gets lost, and the scientists are marooned. Very loosely based on Verne's original story.

Actor and singer Pat Boone as Alec (Axel) in a still from the 1959 Hollywood film of Journey to the Center of the Earth.

1998 Children's feature film, USA.
Two boys and their nanny fall into a volcano in Hawaii.

1999 Film for cable TV, USA.
Follows the start of Verne's story, but then features battles with an underground cannibal tribe.

c.2000 Cartoon version, UK.
In the young children's series, *Adventures of Willy Fogg*.

c.2000 *Journey to the Hollow Earth*, USA.
Not an adaptation of Verne's story, but a TV documentary investigating the belief—still held by some people—that the Earth is hollow.

2003 TV documentary, USA.
Combines scenes from Verne's story with real-life views deep underground.

2006–2007 New version in production, USA.
Said to include stereovision and 3-D special effects.

INDEX

FURTHER INFORMATION

IF YOU LIKED THIS BOOK, YOU MIGHT ALSO WANT TO TRY THESE
TITLES IN THE BARRON'S *GRAPHIC CLASSICS* SERIES:

The Hunchback of Notre Dame
Kidnapped
Moby Dick
Oliver Twist
Treasure Island

FOR MORE INFORMATION ON JULES VERNE:

www.jules-verne.co.uk
www.kirjasto.sci.fi/verne
http://jv.gilead.org.il